Home for Meow

The Purrfect Show

Home for Meow

The Purrfect Show

Reese Eschmann

Scholastic Inc.

Copyright © 2022 by Charisse Eschmann

All rights reserved. Published by Scholastic Inc., *Publishers since 1920.* SCHOLASTIC and associated logos are trademarks and/or registered trademarks of Scholastic Inc.

Library of Congress Cataloging-in-Publication Data available

ISBN 978-1-338-78398-8

10 9 8 7 6 5 4 3 2 1   22 23 24 25 26

Printed in the U.S.A.   40

First edition, July 2022

Book design by Stephanie Yang

Interior art © 2022 by Wendy Tan

Table of Contents

Chapter 1: **Cats and Cake Batter** 1

Chapter 2: **The King County Dog Show** 10

Chapter 3: **Butter and Bracelets** 23

Chapter 4: **Training Day** 41

Chapter 5: **The Trial Run** 57

Chapter 6: **Markers and Mistakes** 79

Chapter 7: **Best in Show** 93

1

Cats and Cake Batter

"I think this is my best idea yet."

Pepper purrs. She leans over the side of the mixing bowl and sniffs the batter inside. Then she licks the tip of her heart-shaped nose. That's how I know this is a *really good* idea.

I, Kira Parker, have a lot of ideas. Some of them

are *pretty good* and some of them are *really good*. My little brother, Ryan, would probably tell you that my ideas are *not so good*, but I know he's going to love this one. After all, who doesn't love cupcakes and cats?

Our family owns The Purrfect Cup, the best and only cat café in town. We live right upstairs, in an apartment with blue walls and yellow tiled floors. Mama runs the business and takes customers' orders. Dad bakes the treats we sell. And I get to spend all day with the best friends a girl could have: the cats!

Pepper, our family's cat, rubs her gray-and-white fur against my arm. I know she's asking for a taste of the batter in my mixing bowl.

"This is for the customers, Pepper," I say. "You know cats can't eat chocolate."

Pepper wears a name tag that I made for her. It says, *Kira's BFF for all 9 lives*. On the back, it has her name and Mama's phone number. Making special name tags was a *great idea* I had in June.

But now it's July, and I have a new idea.

The other cats who live in the café are from the local animal shelter. Customers come to The Purrfect Cup for a mug of tea and a slice of Dad's sweet potato pie. They *stay* because they fall in love with the cats. Sometimes, they decide to adopt a cat and take it home! It's hard to say goodbye to my friends, but I know it's good for them to find their forever homes. Every time a cat gets adopted, Mama, Dad, Ryan, and I throw a party for the customers and give away free mini donuts.

My *new idea* is going to get more people to adopt cats. I'm going to make a cupcake inspired by every cat living at The Purrfect Cup! I'm working on the first cupcake recipe now. It's inspired by Tiger, a striped tabby cat.

For this recipe, I need two types of batter. Tiger is sweet and round, like an orange, so the first flavor is orange cream cake. Tiger can also act a little bitter when I wake her up from her naps. Dark chocolate is bitter too, so the second flavor is dark chocolate.

I swirl the orange and chocolate batters together to make a cupcake striped like Tiger's fur. The swirled batter looks so pretty as I scoop it into the cupcake pan.

"*Everyone* will want to adopt her after they eat this!" I say. "But I wish you all could help me fill these pans. It's hard to scoop the batter without spilling."

Tiger rolls onto her back and licks her paw.

"At least you know to wash your hands before you touch the food," I laugh.

The kitchen is in a separate room behind the café. The oven is three times bigger than the regular one in our apartment upstairs. Dad lets me practice my baking down here as long as I don't turn on the oven without him around. I told him I'd need his help in a few minutes—I'm going to surprise him with my new idea!

Just then Tiger flops back over onto her belly. She sits up in front of the mixing bowl, leans her head back, and lets out a HUGE sneeze! The sound startles Pepper, who leaps over the mixing bowl. Only she doesn't quite make it over—her back paws and her tail dip into the batter!

"Oh no," I say. "Everyone, calm down! I'm sure Tiger just had a tickle in her nose. No reason to panic."

But it's too late. Max, a leopard-spotted kitten who's always looking for trouble, jumps onto the counter. He pounces on a bottle of vanilla extract. Then he goes for the cake batter stuck to Pepper's tail.

"Max, no!" I cry. I reach out for him, accidentally knocking over the mixing bowl. Now I have orange batter all over my apron. *Uh-oh.* I stick a finger in it to see if it at least tastes good.

Suddenly the door to the kitchen swings open.

"Are you kidding me?" Dad asks.

"Don't you mean, are you *kitten* me?" I ask. Dad crosses his arms. Pepper gives me the side-eye. I should have known a cat joke wouldn't get me out of this mess.

"Kira, what did I say about cats in the kitchen?"

"You said no unsupervised cats in the kitchen."

Dad sighs. "I said no cats in the kitchen. *Period.* I can't have cat hair getting into my homemade marshmallow fluff."

"I'm sorry," I say. "I'll help you clean up!"

I turn around to pick up the bottle of vanilla extract and accidentally knock over the baking powder.

Dad's face crumples into a grumpy scowl.

"That's okay, Kira. Why don't you go help your mama out in the café?"

I scoop Tiger into my arms. Max leaps onto my shoulder.

"C'mon, guys," I say. "I'll have to come up with a new idea to help you get adopted."

2

The King County Dog Show

The Purrfect Cup is my favorite place in the whole world. There are rows of comfy green seats where customers sip tea while cats sit on their laps. In front of the big window looking out onto the street are baskets lined with soft blankets. My cat friends love to cuddle there when they're not chasing yarn balls.

At the back of the café is the bakery case where Dad stores all the sweets. It's right next to the register where Mama takes customers' orders.

But she's not standing there now.

Max leaps off my shoulder and scratches at the glass covering the baking case.

"No, you can't have a kiwi tart," I say. "I wonder what Mama's doing at the front of the café."

In fact, it seems like everyone in the café is standing near the front. My little brother, Ryan, has his nose pressed up against the window. His bright blue sneakers perfectly match the blue stripe running along the side of his pants. Mama, Dad, and I always wear clothes that can get dirty in the café, but Ryan never has a speck of cat hair on him. I look down at my dirty white sneakers. There's cake batter on them. *Oh well.* I'll get Pepper to lick it off later.

I walk up to Ryan.

"What are you all looking at?" I ask.

"This corgi!" he says. "He's amazing."

I look out the window and see a dog with a long, round body and little legs.

Tiger jumps out of my arms and curls up inside one of the baskets. She can't be bothered with dogs.

"What's so amazing about it?" I ask.

"Just watch," says Ryan.

The dog's owner points at the sky. The corgi

leaps into the air! Then, the owner turns in circles, and her dog turns with her. It looks like they're dancing. Ryan laughs.

"Dogs are so cool!" he says. "They're way more fun than cats."

I cross my arms. "Take that back. You *love* cats."

"I do not!" Ryan says.

"Then why are you holding two of them?"

Ryan looks down at the kittens sleeping in his arms. Nora and Zora are twins who just came to live at The Purrfect Cup. Ryan hasn't let them out of his sight all week.

Ryan pouts. "I'm only holding them because they would cry if I didn't—whoa, what's she going to do with that?"

I look back at the corgi. Its owner pulls a jump rope out of her pocket. She and the corgi jump together. The rope sweeps beneath their feet.

Everyone in The Purrfect Cup cheers! The corgi and her owner turn toward the window. The owner bows, then the corgi stands up on its hind legs and bows too. They turn and walk down the street. Near the door, Mama turns to her friend Mrs. Patel.

"That was very impressive," Mama says.

Mrs. Patel takes a sip of her tea. She comes to

The Purrfect Cup every day, but she always brings her tea from home and stands near the door. Apparently she's allergic to cats.

"The corgi is supposed to take first place," Mrs. Patel says. "But there's a rumor that a new Saint Bernard might win."

"Win what?" I ask.

Mama looks at the batter splattered on my apron and my shoes. She raises an eyebrow, then goes back to talking to Mrs. Patel. *That's weird.* She didn't even ask me how I got so messy!

"First place in *what*?" I ask Mama again.

"The King County Dog Show!" My human friend Alex Patel steps out from behind her mom. I smile when I see her. Alex is the best kind of human. She's always in a good mood. My cats love coming up to her because she never startles them like some people do. Alex wears jeweled cat-eye glasses and a bracelet covered in green stones.

"Hey, Alex," I say. "I didn't see you there. What's this dog show about?"

"It's a competition to see which dog knows the best tricks. The best dogs from all over the county come to compete. They usually have it in the city, but this year they decided to have it here in Bloomington! It's on Saturday, but Mom says it's going to be the talk of the town for *months*. Lots of reporters are coming."

Alex's mom, Mrs. Patel, knows everything about our town. If she says it will be the talk of the town, she's probably right. I look down at Tiger snoozing in her basket.

"Aren't you excited?" Alex says. "You love animals!"

"I love our *cats*. They're my friends. Who will adopt them if everyone is busy talking about dogs?"

"Hmm, that's a good point," Alex says.

Alex always tells me I have a *good point* when I share my thoughts. It lets me know she's listening.

"Well, what are you going to do?" Alex asks.

"What do you mean?"

"This seems like a time for one of your *great ideas.*"

Pepper meows at my feet. Her tail and paws are clean again. Looks like Dad got all the batter off. I pick her up. She gently paws at the colorful beads that loop over my twists. I love it when she does that. Pepper is my best friend and the perfect cat. She's soft and sweet and super smart. Suddenly I get an idea. That corgi isn't the only one who's smart enough to know a few tricks!

"You're right!" I say to Alex. "I know how to get everyone to care about the cats again. Will you help me?"

Alex nods. I whisper in her ear. Then I run to grab a handful of kitty treats. Alex tugs on her mom's shirt and asks her to get everyone's attention.

Mrs. Patel's voice is deep and loud, and she never misses a chance to talk to everyone at once.

"Excuse me!" she calls out. Every head in the café turns to look at her. "I need everyone's attention, please. My daughter has something to say."

"Actually," Alex giggles nervously. She doesn't like getting lots of attention—unless it's from the cats. "My friend Kira has something to show you."

I take a deep breath and set Pepper on the ground next to me. First, I let her sniff the treats in my hand. Then I cross to the other side of the café. Pepper and I have been best friends for three years. We've had lots of time to learn tricks from each other.

"Pepper, come!" I say. Pepper walks over to me,

swishing her long tail. She's a lot more graceful than the corgi. I give her a treat.

"Pepper, sit pretty!"

She sits and turns her head to one side, letting everyone see her shiny fur and her beautiful golden eyes. I hear gasps from the customers, and someone yells, "Awwww!"

I smile. Now for the grand finale.

I crouch down in front of her and lift my hand.

"Pepper," I say. "High five!"

She stares at my hand for several seconds, like she's making up her mind. Then she lifts her paw and presses it against my palm. I *knew* she wouldn't let me down!

The customers cheer. Even Mama looks impressed. I carry Pepper around and let the customers admire her.

"She's so beautiful," says a boy with a quiet voice. He smiles shyly.

"I didn't even know cats *could* be trained," the man next to him says. "I'm Mr. Perez, and this is my son, Isaac. This is our first time at the café. We didn't realize the cats would be so talented!"

"I know," I say. "They're the best."

And then I get the *best idea ever*. Getting a great idea is like making cupcakes. It starts with thoughts sitting in separate bowls. *Dogs. Tricks. Talk of the town.* Then my thoughts mix together like flour, sugar, and eggs. I put the idea into my brain-oven and it grows, like scoops of cake batter puffing up into cupcakes.

My cats *are* as talented as that corgi—maybe even more talented. And I'm going to prove it.

My cats are going to win the King County Dog Show.

3

Butter and Bracelets

"Our cats? In the *dog* show?" Mama asks. She places one of her long nails against her chin. She always does that when she's thinking.

"It's a perfect idea!" I say. "My very best. Once people see our cats win the dog show, they'll come adopt them! Here, let me help you while you think."

I offer to help because I want to butter Mama up. Dad told me all about buttering people. You do something nice for them so they'll listen to your ideas. So helping Mama is like smearing a pat of golden butter onto a stack of pancakes. It makes Mama more likely to agree with me, just like butter makes pancakes more likely to agree with my stomach.

Other things are better with butter too. Like the box of rich, lemony shortbread cookies Mama sets on top of the pastry case.

"Thanks, Kira," Mama says. "Mr. Anderson said he was going to come pick these up. But it would be nice if you dropped them off. I saw a big delivery go to the art store today. He must be busy."

"No problem," I say. "It's my pleasure. I'll be right back and we can talk about the show!"

I make my voice extra smooth and sweet. Like butter, my good ideas are hard to resist.

Mr. Anderson owns the art shop right next door to The Purrfect Cup. He is also one of my favorite customers. He comes to the café every day to see the cats and buy something for his sweet tooth. Once, Ryan asked him which tooth was sweet. Mr. Anderson said it was the front left tooth. I think all my teeth might be sweet. These lemon cookies sure smell good. I grab them and turn toward the door.

Now that the corgi is gone, the customers at The Purrrfect Cup are back at their regular tables. The cats are lying in baskets and chasing rays of sunlight that come through the window. As I walk out, I spot Tiger sitting on a shelf near the door. She's playing with Alex's beaded brace-let. Alex must have dropped it earlier.

"Tiger, where did you find that? If you give it to me, I'll let you come on my delivery."

Tiger is one of Mr. Anderson's favorite cats. Or maybe Mr. Anderson is one of Tiger's favorite people. Either way, I bet Mr. Anderson would love cookies *and* a visit from a cat! I tuck the box of cookies under my right elbow and put the brace-let in my pocket to give to Alex later. Then I scoop Tiger up with my left arm. The bells on the door to The Purrfect Cup ring as we leave the café.

Outside, I can see all the colorful shops on Main Street. Ours is the prettiest. The brick wall is painted blue as the sky. Above the shop, there's a big painting of a cat sitting in a teacup next to letters that spell *The Purrfect Cup*. Our apartment is just above the painting. I can see my bedroom window from here. My curtains are made out of pink fabric printed with black cats. I got the fabric from Mr. Anderson's shop because he had some left over from a project. Sometimes he lets me try new markers and pens at the shop too. I hope he has markers today. I like to draw when I'm feeling nervous, and right now I feel like I've got a hair ball in my stomach. I really hope Mama lets the cats enter the dog show.

The sign above the art shop says *Anderson's Artsy Abode.* Inside, the shop is small and cozy. If I stand on my tiptoes, I can see all the shelves lined with bright markers and bottles of paint. The store smells like wood and roses. Mr. Anderson's husband, Ben, hangs flowers all around the shop. One time I had a great idea to put flower pots on the tables at The Purrfect Cup. Tiger knocked every pot over, and Max wanted to eat the flowers. I had to clean up a lot of dirt that day.

Mr. Anderson smiles when he sees us. Tiger leaps out of my arms and hops up onto the counter. She purrs and leans into Mr. Anderson's hand for a good behind-the-ears scratch.

"Kira!" Mr. Anderson says. "I was hoping to see

you. And not just because you're carrying my

cookies."

"Hi, Mr. Anderson," I say. I set the box of cook-

ies on the counter. "Do you have any new markers

you want me to try out?"

"Actually, I have something else," he says, "It's

a new printer that makes posters. I thought we could print some of your art to test it."

"Awesome," I say. "Last week Ryan said Pepper sheds too much, so I drew a portrait of him with fangs. It would look great as a poster!"

"That sounds, uh, interesting. But we can decide later. Do you want a cookie?"

"Sure!" I say. I take a cookie from the box and bite down. The buttery shortbread melts in my mouth. "Thanks. If you don't mind, I'm going to stay here for a minute while I wait for Mama to think about my new idea."

"Ah, I see. Want to tell me about it?" Mr. Anderson asks.

I nod. "I'm going to enter my cats into the

King County Dog Show to help them get adopted! And because I think they can beat all those smelly dogs. Hopefully Mama says it's okay."

"Now, *that's* an idea," Mr. Anderson chuckles. He stops Tiger from jumping into one of the flowerpots. "Tell you what. If your mom and the people who make the dog show rules say it's okay, you can print some posters for the show here. How's that sound?"

"That's a GREAT idea!" I shout. Tiger hunches her back and leaps onto the floor. She doesn't like loud noises. "Oops, sorry, Tiger."

I lean down to pick her up. Mama should be buttery enough by now.

"Thanks, Mr. Anderson," I say. "I'm going to go tell Mama right away!"

He smiles and pops a cookie into his mouth as I race back to the café. I start shouting before I even get the door open. "Mama! Mr. Anderson said I could print posters for the King County Dog *and* Cat Show at his shop. Once everyone knows our cats are going to be in the show, we'll be the talk of the town!"

"Kira, *shhh*! Mrs. Patel is on the phone."

Oops. I didn't notice that Mrs. Patel and Alex were back at the café. And for once, Mrs. Patel isn't standing by the door. She's all the way up at the counter with Mama! Something must be going on.

I hand Tiger to Alex and lean over the counter to get close to Mama.

"I decided the cat show is a *great* idea," Mama whispers. I bounce up and down on my toes. I can't believe this is really happening. This idea baked up better than any of my cupcakes. I can almost taste our victory! Mama seems to feel the same. She says, "Entering the cats in a big event like this will bring visibility to our café. Increased visibility means more customers, bigger profit margins, and most importantly—more adoptions, like you said."

"Eggs-actly," I say. I didn't understand everything she said. But the idea of more customers and more adoptions is *great*! "So we can join? Mr.

Anderson said we can print posters at his shop!"

"Well, it's not that easy," Mama whispers. "We have to get special permission. I'm not sure cats have ever entered a dog show before."

Alex leans in close to me. "So when we came back to The Purrfect Cup to look for my bracelet, your mom asked my mom to work her magic."

Mrs. Patel turns around and winks. She says, "Yes, of course, I understand," into her phone in her most buttery voice. She has the magical power of being friends with everybody. I know she'll be able to convince the dog people that they should become cat people too.

I pull the bracelet out of my pocket and hand it to Alex. "One problem solved, one to go!"

Tiger paws at the stones on the bracelet. She still thinks it's a toy!

"Tiger, stop! Tiger, calm down!"

Tiger looks me right in the eye and keeps pawing at the bracelet.

"You have a lot of work to do if you're going to be in the cat show," I say, frowning.

Alex giggles. She takes the bracelet and sits down on a cushion on the floor. She crosses her legs and places her hands in her lap. I plop down next to her.

"Do you think the dog show will be on TV?" Alex asks. "I'd hate to be on television. Too many people watching. I don't know how the dogs do it."

"What? You'd be great on TV!" I say. "I bet you

would stay calm and wouldn't mix up any words at all. Remember that time I had the idea to make a movie? I couldn't remember any of my lines!"

Alex laughs. "That was a fun idea. I liked figuring out how my mom's camera works."

I look around at the cats. "The cats won't worry about too many people watching them on TV," I say. "They don't care much what people think about them."

Tiger jumps from a chair to a shelf on the wall, never taking her eyes off the green stones on Alex's bracelet.

"And Tiger is focused," Alex says. "That's very important."

"You're right," I say. "Maybe we should find

out everything the cats will need to do."

"Good idea," says Alex.

"Here you go, girls," whispers Mama. She leans over the counter and hands us her laptop.

Alex finds the King County Dog Show rules. She's really good at learning new things. "The cats will need handlers to walk around with them. And they'll be judged on their poses—"

"Easy-peasy! I'll be the handler, and they already have beautiful poses. Look at Pepper."

Pepper is sitting on a chair nearby, cleaning her paws. She stops mid-lick when she hears her name and gives me a wide-eyed stare.

"And they'll be judged on their gait."

"What's a gait?" Ryan's voice pops up in my

ear. He plops down next to us. "By the way, I think this is a terrible idea."

"I'm going to ignore that. Also, you have chocolate crumbs all over your face." I turn away from him. "What *does* 'gait' mean, Alex?"

Alex looks up the meaning of gait. "It's the way the dogs walk. In the show, the dogs walk around next to their handlers and do obstacle courses and stuff."

"See? A terrible idea," Ryan says. "Cats don't care about obstacle courses. They care about naps."

"That's only because they've never been invited to the obstacle course before. They're so smart, they'll figure it out right away. They're always climbing on stuff at the café. This is a *great idea!*"

Ryan shrugs. He wipes the chocolate crumbs off his face. He just likes disagreeing with me. But we do have a lot of work to do. Pepper is going to need to learn a lot more tricks than "come," "sit," and "look pretty" if she's going to do an obstacle course. And the show is only five days away. I place my hand on my stomach. I still feel the hair ball in there.

Just then Mrs. Patel spins around in a circle. She says, very loudly, "Thank you! We'll see you on Saturday!" and hangs up the phone.

I stand up straight. "You'll see who on Saturday?"

"Ms. Sato, the King County Dog Show coordinator. She's an old friend."

"Yes!" I shout. Alex cheers and Mama puts her hands up in the air.

The door to the kitchen opens. Dad brings out a tray of chocolate cupcakes.

"Couldn't help overhearing what you all have been up to," he says. "I baked a special treat for the occasion."

I run over to grab a cupcake. Dad used blue frosting to put a ribbon on top of each one.

"The blue ribbon means *Best in Show*," he says.

"Perfect." I pick up a cupcake and take a huge bite. The chocolate cake is rich and tender. I like the taste of being Best in Show.

Now I need to make sure we actually win.

4

Training Day

Yellow sunshine lights up the café's chairs and tables. Max is sleeping on top of the empty counter. The morning light makes rainbows that bounce off a mirror on the wall. Tiger paws at the colors. We always open late on Tuesdays. Mama and Dad sleep in—but only until seven in the morning. Then we eat stacks of blueberry pancakes until the customers start to show up.

I get ready for Training Day while Dad makes pancakes. I push all the tables to the right side of the café. I'm sure the customers won't mind sitting close to each other. They'll probably all become friends, then they'll want to come by the café even more! I should have thought of this earlier.

Yesterday, Mrs. Patel told me a woman named Ms. Sato is in charge of the dog show. Ms. Sato agreed to change some of the show rules for the cats. They only have to do part of the obstacle course. I think they could do the whole thing, but Alex reminded me the dogs had more time to train than we do. Mama helped me type a list of things they will need to learn.

King County Dog and Cat Show—New Rules

1. Four cats will participate in the King County Dog and Cat Show. Each cat must have a handler who walks next to them at all times.

2. There will be a beauty contest and an agility contest. Dogs and cats will compete for Best in Show. One of the cats will also win a separate prize for Best in Breed!

3. For the agility contest, cats must jump through a hoop, walk on a balance beam, and run through a tunnel. (Reminder for future Kira: Agility means you can move fast and easily.)

I love seeing *and Cat* in the King County Dog Show name. It makes me feel very official. Like

I'm officially the greatest at coming up with ideas. And Mrs. Patel said I can show off Pepper's tricks during the beauty contest. No other animal will be able to sit as pretty as she does! I'll be Pepper's handler, of course. BFFs have to stick together. Mama, Ryan, and Alex will be the other handlers, but they haven't picked their cats yet.

Just then Max jumps onto a long piece of wood on the floor and scratches it.

"Max, be gentle! You won't be able to go to the dog show if you scratch all our new stuff."

Last night when the shop closed, Dad took me to the store to get wood for a balance beam. We also borrowed a Hula-Hoop and a bright-colored tunnel from the preschool down the street.

Now, I set everything up on the left side of the café. Ryan comes downstairs from our apartment. He looks like he just woke up. There's crust in the corners of his eyes and his hair is flat on one side. He hasn't even put on his sneakers-of-the-day yet.

"Can you help me balance this piece of wood on two chairs?" I ask.

"No," he grumbles. "I'm still asleep."

Ryan bends down anyway and lifts a corner of the wood. He yawns loudly.

"I'm glad there's no King County Human Show," I say. "You'd have a hard time in the beauty contest."

Ryan narrows his eyes. "When Dad brings out

pancakes, I hope you get the one with the least blueberries."

I ignore him. "Which cat will you choose? Nora or Zora?"

"Nora and Zora are too young to compete," Ryan says. He walks over to look inside the basket where the two of them are snuggled up together. "If they lose, it might hurt their feelings. I don't want them to be upset. I think an older cat will have a better chance."

"I thought you said this was a terrible idea. Now you think a cat *could* win."

Ryan crosses his arms. "That's not what I said! The dogs are going to kick our butts."

"No way," I say. "Dogs are too goofy. Our cats

are smart and graceful. This is going to be easy as pie."

"Uhh, Kira, last time you baked a pie it exploded in the oven."

"Yeah, but Pepper and Max loved licking the apple filling that spilled. So it still counts."

Ryan shakes his head. "Cats shouldn't have sugar. It's bad for their tummies."

I sigh. "If Nora and Zora aren't going to compete, maybe you should let them play in the cardboard box."

Ryan makes a face at me, scoops up Nora and Zora, and walks away.

There is a knock on the door at the front of the café. Through the glass, I see Alex and Mrs. Patel!

But they're not alone. The boy who was at the café yesterday, Isaac, is back with his dad, Mr. Perez.

Mama comes down from our apartment. She waves at the morning's first customers.

"Hey, Alex, come on in. I'm glad you're training with Kira today. Mrs. Patel, do you want something to go?"

"Oh, no, thank you," Mrs. Patel says, pointing at her mug. "I better not come inside. My allergies are acting up after I was in here yesterday. Have fun, Alex! I'll pick you up in a few hours."

Mrs. Patel rubs her nose and walks away.

Mama looks at Isaac and Mr. Perez. "Good morning! I'm sorry, the café doesn't open until nine o'clock today."

I step forward. "Mama, this is Isaac and his dad, Mr. Perez. They're new to town. I bet they didn't know we open late on Tuesdays. Could they stay? I think we have enough pancakes."

Mama smiles warmly. "Of course. Good idea, Kira. Always good to meet new neighbors. Come on in! I hope you like blueberries."

Mr. Perez squeezes Isaac's hand. "Thank you so much. We like eating *everything*."

My kind of people! I smile.

♥ 🐾 ♥

After we finish our pancakes, Mama and Dad get the café ready to open. Isaac and Mr. Perez sit down to watch Training Day.

I grab a handful of kitty treats and the cats all

come running! Pepper and Max try to climb up my leg, and Tiger crawls onto Ryan's shoulder.

"Wait a second!" I say. "No treats yet."

Alex and I set all the cats in a cardboard box. Cats love boxes. They roll around and start playing with each other. That gives me time to get ready.

I set several treats on the wood beam, spacing

them out. This way, the cats will have to walk along the balance beam to eat all the treats. Then I'll put treats in the tunnel. It's the perfect training plan! I get Pepper out of the box. She hops up onto the wood beam right away. That'll show Ryan. I *knew* this would be easy.

Pepper walks across the beam to reach the first treat. Her tail swishes gracefully behind her. There's no dog in the world that can balance on a beam like my cats do. Pepper reaches the first treat and bends down to sniff it.

"Good job, Pepper!" I say, but I speak too soon.

Pepper turns her head away from the treat.

"Wait, Pepper!" I say. "These are your favorites. Don't you want it?"

She rolls onto her back and wiggles around on the beam.

"I think she's giving herself a back scratch," Ryan says.

On the other side of the room, Isaac giggles. Pepper sits up when she hears the sound of his laugh. She hops off the beam, crosses the room, and rubs her back against Isaac's leg. He freezes.

"Isaac, are you okay?" Mr. Perez asks. He looks at me. "Sorry, we're not used to animals. We've never had a pet. But I thought we might like having a furry friend to play with at home. The cat café is a good introduction."

"Of course it is!" I say. "Pepper may not be good at the balance beam, but she's very friendly."

"A little *too* friendly," Ryan grumbles. He walks over and picks Pepper up. I think he just wants her all to himself. She snuggles into his neck.

"Well, looks like Pepper's taking a break from training. Who's next?"

I look into the cardboard box. Tiger is fast asleep, and Max is nowhere to be found.

"Uh-oh," Alex says. "Look at Max."

Max is on the highest shelf in the café, too high for any of us to reach. He sits on a pile of books and tries to bite his own tail.

"Max, come!" I shake the bag of treats. Max stares at his tail like he thinks *his tail* is a treat, and leaps down from the shelf. He bounces around in a circle and tries to grab his tail. *Oh no.*

This is a disaster. Chasing tails won't win us the beauty contest!

Beside me, Alex gasps.

"I know," I say. "What's wrong with Max?"

"No, it's not him—look!"

I look down at the balance beam. Callie, one of our new cats, is walking toward the treat! She came from the shelter two weeks ago, but she's very shy. She spends all day hiding in a basket. I've never seen her come out to play before! She's not as graceful as Pepper, but she's a beautiful cat. She has black fur on one side of her face and orange fur on the other side.

Callie walks across the balance beam, eating every treat. I clap my hands over my mouth.

Callie hops down from the balance beam and walks through the tunnel.

"Ryan," I whisper. "Quick, get the Hula-Hoop!"

I place a treat on the chair closest to Callie. Ryan lifts the Hula-Hoop so that it's in front of the chair, and Callie jumps through! She lands on the chair and happily eats the treat. Everyone claps—Mama and Dad came out of the kitchen just in time to see! Even Max stops chasing his tail so he can watch Callie.

"Who is that?" Isaac asks. "I like the colors on her face."

Isaac stares at Callie, and she stares back at him. She lets out a long purr. Isaac raises an eyebrow.

"That means she likes you!" I say. "This is Callie. She's one of our newest cats."

"She seems like she might be one of your best cats," says Mr. Perez.

"You know, I think you're right."

Training Day One hasn't gone as planned. But at least we found our fourth cat for the show. We have some long training days ahead if we're going to win. But I hold on to the taste of victory, sweet like buttercream frosting. Hopefully Callie can teach the other cats a thing or two. I look at her, and she winks.

We've totally got this.

5

The Trial Run

"Don't stress, do your best!"

Alex whispers in Tiger's ear. She gives her a pat on the head. Tiger purrs and stretches her back legs. She's ready to walk across the balance beam. Alex walks next to her, and Tiger stays close. She crosses the balance beam, walks through the tunnel, and jumps through the hoop

in front of the chair! Tiger rubs against Alex's leg.

"You believed you could, so you did," Alex says

to Tiger.

On Training Day Two, Alex used Mama's laptop

to do a bunch of research on training cats. She's

really good at looking stuff up on the internet. And it turns out, some cats like when people tell them nice things. They don't even need treats! Tiger is one of those cats. She loves Alex's encouraging words as much as she loves Mr. Anderson's head scratches.

Now it's Training Day Four, and things are finally coming together.

"Way to go, Tiger!" I say. "Okay, Max and Ryan's turn."

Ryan marches forward, raising his knees to his chest as he crosses the room, and keeping his arms still by his side. Ryan says he's like an army sergeant and Max is his new recruit. He says Max needs rules and tough love. I didn't read that anywhere on

Mama's laptop, but it seems to work for Max.

Ryan blows a whistle he found in the attic. "Atten-tion!"

Max's ears perk up. He runs over to the balance beam and does the whole obstacle course in less than ten seconds.

"Excellent work, recruit. You're getting promoted." Ryan leans down and gives Max a small piece of banana.

"Now hang on a second." Dad's booming voice crosses the café. "Is that where all my bananas went? I was going to make banana blue ribbon cupcakes for the show."

Ryan gulps. He pulls a brown banana out of his pocket and hands it to Dad.

Dad frowns. "What am I gonna do with half a banana? These spoiled cats. Might as well let them eat it."

Dad breaks the banana into pieces and gives some to Tiger, Max, Callie, and Pepper. The cats lick his hands even after the banana is gone, and I see Dad's eyes soften. Ryan lets out a big sigh. I smile as I turn back to the obstacle course.

"Now Callie and Mama."

Mama comes out from behind the café counter. She is going to be Callie's handler. Even though Callie is the best at the obstacle course, she's still a little shy around humans. Mama had to use treats to get her to come down from a shelf this morning. Callie looked at her suspiciously for a whole five minutes before she decided to join us.

"Go, Callie, go!" says Mr. Perez.

Isaac and Mr. Perez have come to the café every day to watch our training sessions. This morning, Isaac even helped me set everything up.

Isaac claps loudly as Callie and Mama finish the obstacle course. Callie walks over to him and licks his shoe. Isaac freezes. He looks a little nervous. I think he's as shy as Callie.

"Wow, she really likes you, Isaac!" I say. "She's never licked my shoe."

"Well, I did make a tuna sandwich yesterday," he says. "I might have spilled a little on my shoe."

He hesitates, then leans down and gives

Callie a gentle pat on her back. She rubs against his leg. Beside me, Pepper swishes her tail happily. She's ready for her turn!

"Last but not least, me and Pepper." I wave as Mr. Anderson and his husband, Ben, walk into the café. I love having an audience.

The key to training Pepper was to show her how to do the obstacle course myself. She watched me when I walked over the wood, climbed through the tunnel, and jumped through the Hula-Hoop. I had to do it a lot of times, and I'm a little too big for the tunnel. I almost got stuck. But it was worth it!

Pepper does the obstacle course and follows it up with a little practice for the beauty contest.

She swishes her tail and sits pretty for the customers in the café.

Everyone cheers. I look around. Every seat at the café is full. My plan is already working!

Mr. Anderson and Ben walk over to me. They both look very excited.

"What do you think of the posters, Kira?" Mr. Anderson asks. "Once we get your approval, we'll hang them around town." He holds up the poster that Mama and I designed yesterday. It's covered in colorful cat paw prints and blue Best in Show ribbons. I read the poster's bright orange words.

This Saturday, don't miss the first-ever
KING COUNTY DOG
AND CAT SHOW!

**Featuring four fabulous felines from
Bloomington's best cat café,**

The Purrfect Cup!

Post-show adoption fair on Sunday at 2 p.m.

"It's purrfect!" I say, scooping up Pepper and spinning around in a circle. "Thank you so much!"

"That's not all! Go on, show her, Ben!" Mr. Anderson and Ben have huge smiles on their faces.

Ben reveals a bag hidden behind his back. Inside, there are four small triangle-shaped pieces of blue fabric. Ben sewed the words *Visit Me at The Purrfect Cup* onto each one!

"They're kerchiefs to tie around the cats' necks! To increase visibility for the café!" Ben winks at Mama. "They were actually Ryan's idea. He thought the cats should look nice when they're on TV."

"The cats always look nice," I say. Ryan scowls, but when I tie one of the kerchiefs around Pepper's neck, his face goes back to smiling. Pepper tries to bite it and shows me her grumpiest cat face, but that's okay. She looks prettier than ever.

"I can't believe it. I think we're ready for the show!" I say.

"Well, that's good to hear," Mrs. Patel says as she walks into the doorway of the café. "Because I just got off the phone with Ms. Sato. She wants you to go to the arena today for a trial run."

"A trial what, now?" I ask.

"Don't worry," says Mrs. Patel. "It's just a quick meet-and-greet so the cats can see the arena. Ms. Sato thinks it will be good for them to see the obstacle course she has set up."

"That sounds fun, doesn't it, Kira?" Alex asks.

I'm not so sure. I wish we had known about the trial run earlier. Pepper jumps out of my arms and coughs up a huge hair ball.

"You and me both," I say.

One hour later, we arrive at the arena. The cats are each in their own cat carriers. Ryan and I put soft blankets and toys in the carriers so they'd be happy on the drive over. Ryan also tried on three different outfits before deciding to wear his lime green sneakers and a matching baseball hat. He's nervous, but he won't admit it.

The arena is huge and shaped like a circle. There are rows and rows of seats. In the middle of the arena is a big open space covered in green carpet. The obstacle course is already set up—I see the balance beam and tunnel for the cats! There's also a larger obstacle course where dogs are running around. They are *fast*.

The corgi that was outside our shop is doing his tricks with his handler in the corner. There's a big box covered in carpet near us. A huge, shaggy black dog with white-and-brown fur on her face is sitting on it. She's having her picture taken.

"I bet that's the new Saint Bernard my mom was talking about," Alex whispers.

"Right you are!" I turn around to see who answered. A woman in a black suit appears behind us. She talks very fast. "Hello, hello, I'm Ms. Sato! Ah, look at these precious kitties! I'm so glad you all could make it. Sorry for the late notice. Believe me, we are so excited to have cats at this year's dog show. I'm sure everything will run smoothly—these dogs are the most well-behaved dogs in the county! And I've heard your cats are really something. We're already causing quite the buzz on the internet."

"We have posters too," I say, holding one up.

"Oh my, those are precious. Jeffrey, can you get

a picture of those?" Ms. Sato snaps at the man taking pictures of the Saint Bernard. He runs over and starts clicking his camera.

We follow Ms. Sato to the obstacle course. As we walk by, I see the Saint Bernard's head turn toward us. She starts wagging her tail so hard it smacks against her handler's knees. Two more dogs with golden fur also stop what they're doing to stare at us. One of them whines, and the other sticks its tongue out. *Uh-oh.*

"Uh, Ryan," I say. "Why are all the dogs staring at us?"

"They're probably looking at me and thinking I'd be a great dog owner." The corgi in the corner barks twice. "See? He's saying, 'Someone get that guy a puppy!' Hear that, Mama?"

"Now what would Nora and Zora say if you told them you were replacing them with a puppy?" Mama says.

That makes Ryan go quiet. He would never abandon Nora and Zora.

Mama sets the cat carriers on the ground. I put a treat in each carrier while Ryan sets up treats on the balance beam.

Alex kneels in front of Tiger's carrier. "Remember, Tiger," she says in a sweet voice. "Don't stop until you're proud."

She picks Tiger up and places her on the balance beam. Tiger's eyes are wide. She looks around the arena. Her eyes lock on the corgi. He stares back at her, his tail wagging hard. His owner gives him a few commands, and even tugs on his leash. But the corgi doesn't move. He only has eyes for Tiger.

"Tiger, whatever you do, always give one hundred percent," says Alex.

"Right now Tiger is giving one hundred percent to that corgi," I say. "Mama, how about giving Callie a turn?"

Ms. Sato chuckles. "That's funny. Jeffrey, are you getting pictures of this?"

Mama opens Callie's carrier, but Callie is sitting in the back of the cage. When Mama tries to pull her out, she plays dead! Ms. Sato taps her foot impatiently.

"Uh, Ryan," I say quickly. "Let's get Pepper and Max out!"

We open their carriers, but then the Saint Bernard and her handler walk up to us.

"Hey, cat people!" The Saint Bernard's handler waves at us. "My Lucy just can't stop staring at you. She sees someone and immediately thinks she's got new friends."

I do like new friends. I guess up close Lucy is kind of cute, even if she is stinky. When I was little I used to pet puppies that walked by the café. But then Pepper became my best friend, and I got worried she would smell dog fur on me and get jealous. I look at Pepper now. She's still in the carrier with her back turned to me.

Maybe if she feels jealous, she will want to impress me by doing the obstacle course.

"Can I pet Lucy?" I ask.

"Yes, of course! She loves everyone. We even have two cats and a bunny at home!"

"That's cool," I say. I lean down and slowly reach out my hand. Lucy pants so heavily she looks like she's smiling. I scratch her under her chin. Her fur is thick and fluffy. *Maybe dogs aren't so bad,* I think. Then I feel something wet on my hand. Lucy is drooling all over me!

"Ewww," I say, pulling my hand away.

"Sorry," says her owner. "She must smell food on you!"

I frown. "I only smell like cats. And our cats aren't food—"

"Arooooooooo!" One of the dogs with golden fur howls and interrupts me. I turn just in time to see him running across the room toward us.

"Jeffrey, are you getting this? That golden wants to join our party! That's hilari—oh dear!"

The golden runs fast, but he looks so goofy. He's got none of Pepper's grace. He jumps over the balance beam and slides into my feet. He lies on the ground, belly up, and twists his head around to look at all the cats. So much for the most well-behaved dogs in the county! The dog's handler blows a whistle at him, but he keeps rolling around on the carpet.

Pepper sticks one paw out of her carrier and—

SMACK! She pops the golden right on his nose.

It only makes him look happier. Pepper creeps

slowly out of the carrier. She walks up to the

golden and presses both of her paws against his

back. She stares right at me while she kneads her

paws into his fur like Dad kneads dough for

bread. I can't tell if she's trying to play, give

the golden a massage, or get him to go away! I

do know that we need to take control of this

situation.

"Ryan, use your whistle!" I say.

He yells, "Hey, animals! Atten-tion!"

Ryan blows into the whistle. Lucy the Saint

Bernard gets so excited she pulls away from her

handler and runs up to Ryan. Max hears the whistle too. He jumps on top of the carrier, then onto the Saint Bernard's back!

Lucy takes off, with Max riding her like a person rides a horse. The other dogs can't help themselves—they chase Lucy and Max around the obstacle course! They knock over

everything—all the balance beams, Hula-Hoops, and tunnels. *Oh no!* This is more of a disaster than Training Day One.

Ms. Sato looks around at the chaos, then down at Pepper, who's decided to take a nap on top of the golden dog.

"Oh dear," she says. "I'm not sure a dog and cat show was such a good idea after all."

6

Markers and Mistakes

No one speaks on the car ride home. When we

get back to The Purrfect Cup, we set the cats in

the baskets lined with soft blankets. They look

happy to be home. I give Pepper a kiss on her

head and she purrs.

Alex pets Tiger and says, "It's not whether

you get knocked down. It's whether you get back up." She looks at me. "Sorry the dog and cat show didn't work out, Kira. I thought it was a great idea."

"Thanks, Alex. I'm sorry your mom worked all her magic for nothing."

"It's okay. She had fun. I'll go home and look up some more motivational phrases. Just in case Tiger is still feeling down tomorrow. She really wanted to win."

"So did I."

Alex smiles at me sadly as Mrs. Patel waves at her from the doorway. They leave.

I wrap my arms around my middle. I feel heavy and sad. Ryan walks over carrying a cardboard box. Nora and Zora peek their heads out from inside.

"Hey," he says.

"You were right," I say. "The dog show wasn't my best idea. It was a mistake."

"It's not your fault. It's just cats and dogs. They're like apples and oranges."

I sigh. "I never understood that. I like when Dad puts both apples and oranges in his fruit salad."

"Yeah, me too. But I guess we better not get a puppy. I'm stuck with Nora and Zora."

Ryan doesn't look too upset about that. Nora stands up on her back paws and swipes at his nose. He laughs. Even though Ryan thinks my ideas are terrible, he's my best little brother. And he did a good job training Max with his military marching. I wish they could be in the show.

I watch Mama pull the posters off the café windows. Words float around in my head, like an idea falling apart. *Increased visibility. More sales. More adoptions.* None of that will happen now. I wish I had another *great idea* to help our cats get adopted, but I'm not sure I can cook anything up right now. I sigh.

"What's for dinner?" I ask Ryan.

"I don't know," he says. "But I hope it's cupcakes."

"Me too."

My *great idea* didn't end up coming out of the

oven like a perfectly baked cupcake. It feels more like that time I put too much milk in the cake batter and my cupcakes sank in the middle. But at least those still tasted good. Right now there's a sour taste in my mouth, like a hair ball soaked in lemon juice.

Dinner isn't cupcakes, but Dad tries to cheer me up with my favorite mac and cheese. Ryan likes to say his favorite food is salad, but it's not. Dad makes a huge bowl of salad for him, but Ryan puts one leaf of lettuce on his plate and fills the rest up with scoops of cheesy noodles.

"I love salad," he says, through mouthfuls of cheese.

I roll my eyes, but the food does make the sour

taste in my mouth go away. Cheese is always a good idea.

♥ 🐾 ♥

In the morning, Ryan and I are lying on the café floor, watching Nora and Zora wrestle, when Dad drags our TV downstairs.

"What are you doing?" I ask.

"Thought we all might want to watch the dog show," he says. The café is mostly empty. Almost everyone in town is at the arena. But Isaac and Mr. Perez are here, and Alex is reading a book in a chair nearby while her mom chats with Mama from the doorway.

Everyone nods in agreement. I sigh. I guess it's okay to have a little more dog in my life.

Without the cats there to distract them, the dogs do great! They're fast and graceful, and some of them do *amazing* tricks. I'm happy for them, but I can't help but feel sad for my human friends and my cat friends again.

"The dogs look awesome," Ryan says. "I wonder where the corgi got her tutu. Do you think the fabric is from Mr. Anderson's?"

I stand up straight. I have an idea for what might make me feel better.

"Mama, can I go to Mr. Anderson's to see if I can use some markers? Maybe I'll draw a picture of Max riding that stinky Saint Bernard."

I watch as Lucy runs around the obstacle course. She looks almost as graceful as Pepper.

"I'll come with you," Ryan says. "I want to see if Mr. Anderson has some string for Nora and Zora to play with."

We walk over to Mr. Anderson's shop. Ryan carries Nora and Zora in a cardboard box. Ben and Mr. Anderson greet us with sad smiles. I feel relieved that they're not at the arena with everyone else.

"We're so sorry about the dog show," says Ben.

"How did you know? Was it on the news?" I ask.

"Mrs. Patel came by and told us."

"I'm sorry we weren't able to use your posters. Mama was really excited to bring new customers into the café tomorrow. Now we won't be able to have the adoption fair."

"That's a real shame," says Mr. Anderson. Behind his glasses, his eyes are kind. "Would you like to test out some of these new gel pens? They have glitter in them."

Mr. Anderson always knows the right thing to say. "Yes, I'd love to! Thanks."

"Do you have any string for the kittens?" Ryan asks. Nora pokes her head out of the box.

"We just got a huge delivery of new fabric," says Ben. "I've been packing up all the old stock to put in the back. You can look through it if you want. I'm sure there are some ribbons the kittens would love."

Ben points at a pile of boxes near the back of the store. I sit on the floor across from Ryan and use one of the boxes as a table while I draw. I use a green sparkly pen to draw the grass at the arena. I decide to make Lucy the Saint Bernard dog purple. She looks much better that way. As the smooth gel ink flows out of the pen, I feel myself start to relax. Or at least, I'd be able to relax if Ryan and the kittens weren't making so much noise.

Nora and Zora pounce from box to box, landing on the bright fabrics inside. Ryan covers them in a long strip of yellow velvet cloth, then pulls it back and yells, "Peekaboo!"

"Ryan," I say. "I'm trying to draw!"

"But isn't this so fun? Look at all this!" Ryan opens another box and pulls out some red fabric that is covered in sequins. He wraps it around

Nora.

"Hmm, I'm not sure this is Nora's color. But I

bet Pepper would look so pretty in a dress like

this!" he says. "Callie would look good in a tutu

like the corgi's. She'd be the fanciest cat in town.

I bet everyone—"

I stand up fast. My brain spins faster than a cat chasing its tail. "Ryan, I just had a GREAT idea! I'm going to tell Mama right away!"

"But I was about to tell you—"

"Come on, Ryan!" I yell. I put the gel pens back on the counter by Ben and Mr. Anderson and run back to The Purrfect Cup. I can feel my new idea whipping up fast, like when Dad beats egg whites until they form stiff peaks.

"Mama!" I say. I push past the customers at the counter so I can talk to her. "I have a great idea!"

"Okay, Kira, why don't you catch your breath while I take this customer's order? Then you can tell me."

I take five deep breaths and start again, more

slowly. "Mama, I was thinking about it. Our cats may not be the best-trained cats in the county. But they *are* good at being perfectly cute. And if we dress them up in Mr. Anderson's old fabric, they'll be the most fashionable cats around! We don't need the King County Dog Show. We can have our own cat fashion show, right here at The Purrfect Cup!"

"A cat fashion show?" the customer asks as she pays for her coffee. "That sounds adorable. When is that happening?"

Mama raises an eyebrow. I gulp. Ryan walks back into the café. His eyebrows are furrowed and he looks mad. I'm not sure why, though. I turn back to Mama.

"What do you think?"

"Well, we did already start advertising a Sunday event with those posters. So people might be expecting something..." I hold my breath as Mama continues. "If Ben and Mr. Anderson say okay, then what's the harm? You know what, Kira, this is better than a great idea. This is *amazing!*"

7

Best in Show

On Sunday morning, I hang three of our brand-new posters in the café window.

Today at 2 p.m., don't miss

THE PURRFECT SHOW!

**A cat-tastic fashion show
brought to you by the fabulous felines
at Bloomington's best cat café,**

The Purrfect Cup!

**In partnership with
Anderson's Artsy Abode,
Bloomington's tip-top one-stop shop
for all your craft supplies.**

Ben and Mr. Anderson agreed to let us use their old fabrics to make outfits for the cats. And they helped us print new posters!

I'm so excited for the fashion show. I think I have eight hair balls in my stomach. I have my favorite sweatshirt on. It has a cat wearing glasses and reading a book on it. Whenever I wear it, it reminds me to focus. But today, even with my lucky sweatshirt, I'm having a hard time.

Dad appears behind me. He looks like he's been

cooking all morning—he has flour dust all over his apron! He raises an eyebrow as he looks around the café. "Kira, I thought you were cleaning the café! We need this place to be spotless."

"I've been cleaning all morning," I protest. "But Max keeps jumping in the dustpan after I sweep. Then I have to start all over. And Pepper is afraid of the mop. So I haven't used it."

Dad watches me pace all around the café. "That's all right, Kira. How are you feeling?"

"I'm feeling...um..." My mind goes blank. I don't know what to say!

"Let me guess," says Dad. "Nervous? Excited? Very happy and very scared?"

"Yep, all of those," I say.

Dad puts his arm around my shoulders. "All right, then. I know something that will help. Sit down and close your eyes."

I toss my broom to the side. "Or maybe I could help you bake! I'm way better at baking than cleaning."

Dad doesn't look so sure about that.

"I promise I won't explode another pie," I say. "Or spill batter everywhere. Or get cocoa powder up your nose."

Dad chuckles. "I had cocoa powder sneezes for three days when that happened." He squeezes my shoulder. "Kira baby, I love you and your exploding pies. But it's okay to relax. You don't have to do any of this by yourself. I already took care of the baking. In fact, I have a surprise for you."

Even Pepper's ears perk up at the word surprise.

I bounce up and down on my toes, but the weight of Dad's hand on my shoulder keeps me from exploding like a pie. I lean into his arm.

"What is it?" I ask. "Can I see?"

"First, close your eyes. Take five deep breaths, then count to ten, real slow. Okay?"

"Whatever it is, I can wait," Ryan grumbles as he and Mama walk into the café. Ryan has been in a bad mood since yesterday. I'm not sure why.

Dad pulls Ryan into his other arm. "Actually, the surprise is for both of you."

Ryan scrunches up his face, but he leans into Dad too. No one can resist Dad's hugs.

Ryan and I both close our eyes and take deep breaths. It makes me feel more relaxed. Maybe now there are only four hair balls in my stomach. Dad's hand moves away as he runs into the kitchen to grab the surprise.

"Okay, you can look!" Dad announces when he's back.

I open my eyes. Pepper jumps onto the café counter and stares as Dad takes a lid off a big silver platter. Inside are dozens of cupcakes. They all have different, beautiful decorations!

"I took your idea and made cupcakes inspired by our cats. Here's the orange-and-chocolate cupcake, for Tiger. And this one has pink frosting just like the tutu Ryan made for Callie. And this last one is for Pepper. It's a red velvet cupcake with red glitter on top because Pepper is going to look fabulous in her new red outfit. Aren't you, my sweet?"

Dad looks emotional as he leans over to pet Pepper.

"Your sweet *who*, now?" I say.

Dad clears his throat. "I meant my sweet Ryan and Kira, of course. I did this for you, not the cats."

"Sure, you did." I take a big bite out of a Tiger-inspired cupcake and smile. Just then the café door swings open. Everyone's here! Mr. Anderson,

Ben, Alex, Mrs. Patel, Isaac, and Mr. Perez all asked to help with the fashion show. I didn't even have to butter them up! I feel ready for the show to get going!

Everyone helps with cleaning and decorating the café. Isaac and Mr. Perez brought an old red rug that was in their new apartment when they moved in. Mr. Perez says if the cats sit on it they will look like movie stars on a red carpet. I have the *great* idea to cut the carpet into squares. We place them around the café in the cats' favorite spots. That way, they'll still look fancy even if all they want to do is nap.

I also put some red carpet on the wood balance

beam. Pepper, Callie, Tiger, and Max can show off what they learned on our training days. When they walk across the balance beam in their fancy outfits, they'll look amazing!

Mrs. Patel stands in the doorway. She tells us all about how the corgi won the beauty contest, the golden dog won the agility contest, and Lucy ended up winning Best in Show yesterday. I feel happy for her, even though she did drool on me. The dogs must be so proud of themselves. I look around at all my friends. I'm proud of us too. Today is our turn to shine as bright as the pups on TV.

"*Mom*," Alex says. "Don't you want to come inside so you can help?"

Mrs. Patel laughs. "You know I help best by talking!"

"Hey, now," says Mama. "That's a good idea! Kira, Ryan, what do you think? Should Mrs. Patel host the show today?"

Ryan mumbles something I don't understand. But I think this is a *great* plan! Now everyone is helping us get ready for the show.

"Teamwork makes the dream work!" Alex says cheerfully. She holds up the shiny purple cat suit that Ben and Ryan were working on.

"Who are you saying that to?" Ryan asks. "Tiger is upstairs in the apartment."

"Um, I guess I like saying the motivational quotes to myself sometimes too," says Alex.

"But this fabric you picked out is perfect for Tiger."

Ben nods. "Ryan has a really good eye for this kind of stuff."

I don't know what that means. Ryan and I got the same score on our eye exams at the doctor's. But Tiger's suit does look great.

"I like it!" I say. "And we do make a good team."

❤ 🐾 ❤

Soon everyone is looking fabulous and *feline* fabulous. The Purrfect Cup looks better than ever! Some of the cats were unsure about sparkles, so we put ribbons and cute collars on them instead.

I pick up Pepper in her pretty red dress and

hold her close. It's almost 2 p.m., but my friends are the only ones in the café. Maybe no one else is coming.

I watch as Mr. Anderson and Ben walk around the café. They can't stop taking pictures of Nora and Zora napping in their matching outfits. When Callie waddles around the room in her pink tutu, Isaac laughs so hard he has to lean on his dad for support. Alex picks up Tiger, and Mrs. Patel gives the cat an awkward pat on the head.

"Kira, why are you smiling?" asks Mama.

"Even if no one else comes . . . I'd say this is a great show."

"Me too," says Mama. She smiles back at me.

I turn to Ryan.

"Is Max upstairs?"

"Yeah," Ryan sighs.

"And you'll bring him down when I give you the signal? So he can do his special trick?"

"Yeah." Ryan doesn't sound excited at all.

"What's going on with you? You seem mad."

Ryan looks like he's been waiting for me to ask that since yesterday. He starts talking fast. "At Mr. Anderson's shop, I pulled out the fabric. Then I told you how it would look good on Pepper, but you interrupted—"

The bell on the door rings. Four people walk in, and then another two behind them. And then three more! I'll have to talk to Ryan later. Mama and I get to work finding everyone a seat. Soon the whole café is full with the sounds of people laughing and admiring our cats!

When there are no seats left, Mrs. Patel begins the show. Her allergies seem to be gone for the day.

"Friends from far and near, welcome to the show of the year! Allow me to introduce you to the fabulous felines of The Purrfect Cup! Please pay special attention to the five cats who are ready for adoption—yes, that means you could take one home today! Here, in this red carpet basket, we have Callie! She is a shy but sweet girl wearing a pretty pink tutu—"

Alex comes over to stand by me while her mom introduces all the cats.

"So fur, so good," I whisper.

"So fur, so *great!*" she agrees.

After Mrs. Patel introduces the cats, it's our time to shine! All our hard work training the cats finally pays off. Pepper, Tiger, and Callie cross the red carpet balance beam. They look so graceful in their outfits, like real cat models! The customers can't believe their eyes! They clap and clap. Then I give Ryan a thumbs-up, and he goes upstairs to get Max for the finale.

Mr. Anderson made Max a special superhero suit. It even has a long blue cape! When Ryan sets him down at the back of the café, Max jumps up onto the red carpet on top of the bakery case! We knew he would. I think Max also has a sweet tooth. His cape flies behind him as he leaps through the air, and everyone cheers!

"Now that your attention is on the bakery case," says Mrs. Patel, "you can see that we have special cat-inspired cupcakes for sale! And you can apply to adopt a cat by talking to Mr. and Mrs. Parker.

"Now let's hear from Kira Parker! It was all Kira's idea to make clothes for these wonderful cats! Without her, we wouldn't have had this amazing show!"

Ryan picks Max up off the bakery case and scowls. He's wearing a suit with bright blue sneakers and a matching blue kerchief in the pocket. It's one of the cat kerchiefs Mr. Anderson gave us for the trial run. They were Ryan's idea. I think about Ben's comment about Ryan's good eye for fabric. Then I think about how Ryan talked about how good Callie would look in a tutu like the corgi's. Suddenly I realize why he's upset! Mrs. Patel waves at me. She wants me to speak to the crowd. I pick Pepper up and walk to the center of the café.

"Hello, everyone, and thank you for coming," I say. "I love our cats more than anything in the world. They are my best friends and they all deserve to find a good home. A place where they fit right in, like they do here. That's why I wanted to do this. But it wasn't my idea."

Ryan stops scowling. He looks surprised.

"My little brother, Ryan, had this idea. He saw this sparkly red fabric. He knew it would make a fabulous outfit for Pepper! Thank you, Ryan. I also want to thank Mama and Dad, and Mr. Anderson and Ben who donated the fabric and made posters! And Mrs. Patel and my best human friend, Alex, who told me and the cats not to give up after we had a bad day. We came up with this idea together, as a team. And I think that makes us Best in Show."

Everyone cheers. Then four customers walk up to the counter to ask Mama about adopting a cat! Ryan and Alex run up to me.

"You didn't have to give me all the credit," Ryan says. "You helped some."

"So," Alex says. "Was this your *greatest idea ever?*"

"I think it was," I say. "But not just because the show went perfectly. This *whole* week has been great! Even the slobbery dog parts. We make a great team."

They both hug me.

Soon everyone is eating cupcakes, and four cats have been adopted. Tiger got adopted by a man with orange hair, and Max jumped right into the arms of a girl wearing a superhero T-shirt. Ryan had a hard time letting go of Nora and Zora, but they were adopted by Ms. Pitcher and Ms. Pitcher—twin teachers at our school who promised Ryan they'd send him pictures of the kittens. Everyone found the perfect home—except for Callie. My heart sinks. She hid behind a basket when too many people were looking at her. Now she might not get adopted. I stand by Mama behind the counter. Isaac and Mr. Perez walk up to me.

"Kira, that was a great show and a great speech! Thank you all for making us feel like we fit in here."

"You do!" says Mama.

"We hope you keep coming for Tuesday pancakes," I say.

"Of course." Mr. Perez takes a deep breath. "And we have something else to say. It's been just the two of us for so long. We've been nervous about adding a new member to the family. What if it isn't the right fit?"

I think I understand what he means. Our cats didn't fit in at the dog show. Changes are scary—and they don't always work out. But in the end, I think it's good to try. We find where we belong. And I belong here, with my cat friends and my human friends. I think Isaac and Mr. Perez belong here too.

Isaac smiles at me. "But we think Callie fits in with us. Our duo is becoming a trio!"

I gasp. My heart explodes like a pie leaving its sticky sweetness all over the café walls. I'm so happy. Callie comes out from behind the basket and hops up onto Isaac's lap. Isaac pets her and she lets out the biggest purr. Mr. Perez can't help but smile.

After Isaac and Mr. Perez leave with Callie, Mama and Dad put their arms around me.

"We're so proud of you," says Mama. "You didn't give up after the dog show didn't work out, and you gave credit to Ryan. That was really nice."

"Well, Alex told Tiger that it's not whether you get knocked down, it's whether you get back up. That was good advice. And it really was Ryan's idea."

Mama and Dad laugh and wrap me in a big hug. I feel warm and full. My stomach is completely hair ball free. But I'm sure the hair balls will be back.

When I get my next *great idea*.

Turn the page for a sneak peek at

Kira's next *great idea* in . . .

Show and Tail

"I'm excited to introduce our class project for this quarter." Ms. Pettina smiles at the class. "We're going to have a pet-themed show and tell right before Thanksgiving!"

I sit up straight in my seat. *Pet-themed show and tell?* Now *this* is my jam. And not just any jam. It's Dad's homemade strawberry jam smeared on a freshly baked biscuit. I get to do a whole project about my cats! Pepper is going to be so excited to meet all my classmates.

A bunch of kids' hands fly into the air.

Ms. Pettina points at a girl sitting in the front row. "Yes?"

"Hello, Ms. Pettina, you might not recognize

me because I didn't go to school in this building last year. My name is Sara."

Ms. Pettina raises her eyebrows again. "Sara, yes, I met your parents at orientation. Do you have a question?"

Sara nods. "What do we do for show and tell if we don't have a pet?"

"There will be lots of options for students who don't have pets. You can write about your favorite animal from a book you've read, or make a presentation on scientific facts about pets."

The rest of the students put their hands down. Ms. Pettina looks around the classroom. "Hmm, did you all have the same question?"

A bunch of my classmates nod. That means they don't have pets, either.

My brain works so fast, I can almost hear it whirring like a blender. Bubbles's kittens are going to need homes. And these kids need pets. I may not be good at solving math problems, but I can already picture my classmates showing their newly adopted kittens to the class. I smile. This is a *great idea*.

Half unicorn, half mermaid, and totally adorable!

Get your fins on all of Lucky's magical adventures!